For Ruth McHale

DRAGON'S BREATH AND YELLOW WELLINGTONS

Written by Chloë Rebecca Bryde

Illustrated by Becca Hall

Tilly was having one of those mornings when everything was just going perfectly.

She had woken up to the sound of her friend, Little Robin, tapping his beak against her bedroom window, followed by a lot of cheerful chirping about something or other.

Most likely, knowing Little Robin, it was to do with good weather; he couldn't stand bad weather.

It wasn't the rain he minded so much, he just couldn't tolerate the colour grey.

Thankfully, today there was only the colour blue spread across the sky, and the sunbeams flooded down on the mountains, making the peaks dance with thousands of sparkles.

It made Tilly smile. It filled her with so much happiness that she sprang from her bed, and before you could say, "hot cross buns," she slid down the banister and sat at the breakfast table, taking a huge bite out of one.

When her mother turned around from the sink, it gave her such a fright to see Tilly suddenly appear. She let go of the hot cross bun she was holding, and it flew as fast as a Frisbee, landing right on Tilly's plate.

"Well, thank you, Mum. I just love seconds!" Tilly said.

Tilly's mum laughed and said, "Good morning, dear," as she poured Tilly and herself a steaming hot cup of tea from the pot.

As Tilly sipped her tea, she looked outside, and her eyes followed the garden path towards the gate. She felt her toes wiggle and her legs start to swing; they were ready to run. She imagined the feeling on the soles of her bare feet on the carpet of green grasses, which she knew led up, up, up into the rugged mountains where she had all her best adventures.

Suddenly, Tilly noticed something she'd never seen before. What looked like huge clouds of thick smoke were pouring out from behind the mountains and were gliding across the still lake.

Tilly was baffled; it didn't make any sense. The day was so sunny. Surely there weren't any clouds? No, this wasn't a cloud, but what was it?

"Pardon, dear!" said Tilly's mother.

Tilly realised that she must have been talking out loud again.

"Those looming clouds of white puff, there," she said, pointing at the ginormous...whatever it was.

"Ah! Well," replied Tilly's mother as she poured herself another cup from the teapot.

Tilly furrowed her brow, which made her nose all wrinkly. This always happened reflexly when adults were being too slow.

Her mother was terrible for it, always thinking about something which was quite irrelevant to the issue at hand.

Tilly's mum saw this face and began to laugh. It did make Tilly look rather adorable! Not in a new-born bunny rabbit way, more like an angry koala bear trying to remove an unwanted party hat from its furry head.

Putting her cup down, Tilly's mother turned and looked at her.

"Well, it's..."

Her eyes widened. "Dragon's breath!"

Tilly's eyes fixed on the breath, which bellowed into the crimson morning sky. Her mind wandered: "Red sky at night, shepherd's delight, red sky in the morning, shepherd's warning."

All the hairs on the back of her neck stood up, and a shiver passed through her body as if a fairy had just whacked her over the head with a lightning bolt.

She imagined the huge black claws of the dragon, squeezing the life out of brave knights like they were lemons being juiced. She thought of the beastie's sharp, glistening teeth as it took a nibble of the passing walkers as though it were gobbling a bag of pick-n-mix sweets.

Oh yes! This dragon was fierce.

One roar could set the whole of Grizedale Forest up in all-consuming flames, and one swish of his daggered scaly tail could turn a field full of cows into 100 steak slices and 50 burgers ready for buns.

Tilly shut her eyes tight in an attempt to stop all the dreadful thoughts, but there, out of the darkness, all she could see were two huge yellow eyes staring back at her.

"Hello, Earth to Captain Tilly! Run upstairs now, lass; your room needs to be tidied up. It looks as if you've had a polar bear staying over."

Tilly climbed the stairs as slow as humanly possible. She considered herself a very tidy person, but she was forever finding her room in a mess. Perhaps there were some monkeys living in the forest who kept breaking in and jumbling everything up. Note to self: Close the window at night!

When she opened the bedroom door, she got the loveliest shock. Everything in the room was exactly where it should be. All her books, which had been scattered across the window ledge, were back in the bookcase, the entire contents of the drawers and wardrobe, which had been on the floor, were now - to Tilly's surprise - back in the drawers and cupboards again.

The tool set and pieces of Tilly's old bicycle, which were in the process of becoming a flying bicycle, had been neatly lined up.

"Who did this?" Tilly thought to herself. Then she noticed the large box sitting on her bed with a big bow, made of newspaper, tied around it.

Tilly smiled to herself. There was no doubt about it; this was definitely the work of her mum.

Tilly ripped open the bow slowly, savouring the soft tearing sound it made in the silence of her bedroom. However, the moment was quickly interrupted by Little Robin, who came flying in through the window, singing at the top of his voice, circling the room four times before settling on Tilly's shoulder.

"Hello, you," she said.

"Just in time, actually. I'm just about to open this box. I can feel it's going to be something very special. Do you want to guess?"

Little Robin tittered in her ear. "A bird box, perhaps. Although I'm not sure I'll fit in it, in any case."

"Let's see," she said, lifting the lid.

Laid on a pile of soft white tissue paper was a beautiful pair of shiny yellow Wellington boots.

Tilly gasped. She had never seen such wonderful things worn on one's feet. It was as if someone had taken all the colours of the daffodils in spring and placed them there, inside the box.

"Mum, I love them. Thank you; thank you."

She was already downstairs, hugging her mum's legs.

"I must go out straight away and wear them everywhere."

"All right," said Mum. "Nothing to do with finding a dragon now, is it?"

A muffled reply came from the pantry as Tilly clattered around, putting things into her rucksack.

"Of course not."

"Here's your flask, and I guess you've already taken those biscuits in the top shelf," said Mum.

"Erm," Tilly chuckled to Little Robin, who had already wrapped them in a bundle and was dropping them into the rucksack.

"Well, be safe," Mum said in valediction.

Tilly jumped up onto a chair and kissed her mum on the forehead.

"Really, you ought to start worrying less, Mum; it's not good for you. See you at supper!"

Tilly shut the red front door and swung on the lion handle, swishing over the plant pots and landing feet down on the garden path.

As she closed the front gate, it made the same little squeak it always did. It sounded as though a little field mouse was stuck inside.

Tilly squeaked back and looked up to see her mum waving from the bedroom window.

Tilly flashed a gleaming smile at her mum, who was trying to say something through the glass, exaggerating the words as she spelt them out. It looked like she was miming eating a very large sandwich to Tilly, who nodded earnestly and skipped off. Tilly had been so busy watching the sun glimmer on her yellow Wellingtons that when she looked up, she was already at the top of the hill. Turning around, she could see her little cottage down past the brook. It looked about the size of a thimble now. Off she went across the meadow, which was covered in all kinds of beautiful flowers. Soon, she reached the stone bridge that crossed the stream, which led into Sheriff's Wood. Tilly crunched through the fallen leaves, kicking them in the air so that they danced around her, falling slowly between the sunbeams; maroon, emerald, and golden brown.

Soon, Tilly found herself deep in the woods. However, the spring seemed very far away, in the dank, dark wildness of the woods. Little Robin stayed very close and listened intently to the rustles and croaks, which repeated like a chorus. Tilly thought it sounded as if the wood had its very own heartbeat. The light was masked by the thick branches of the towering trees, she was definitely getting closer.

Suddenly the sunlight began to shine in between the cracks, making the leaf shadows wriggle about on her raincoat. Finally, she broke through, back in the daylight at last. What a sight! Right in front of Tilly, shooting up out of the grass like a huge ship coming out of the sea, was The Needle; the tallest and most jagged rock in England. "I forgot just how humongous that thing is," said Tilly to herself.

She tilted her head far enough back to glimpse the top. So far back that her head felt as though it was going to drop off into her rucksack. Tilly giggled to herself." That wouldn't do at all," she thought, almost aloud. "Come on, Little Robin.

We'll just have to climb to the top." Little Robin flew around her head like a feathery boomerang.

"All right, all right. Of course, I'll be careful. Anyway, there's really nothing to worry about.

Didn't you see the sticker on the Wellington box?

ANTI SLIP GRIP, PERFECT FOR CLIMBING HUGE ROCKS."

She had to tell Little Robin something, and it was a good job he couldn't read.

Worrying is as much useful as trying to bake a cake by jumping on a trampoline.

So off they went — Tilly, using all her strength to pull herself up, while Little Robin tapped with his beak on the best handhold for her before fluttering off to find the next one. It was a long way to the top, and Tilly noticed that some black clouds had begun to edge across the sky. "Nearly there," she thought. "Best not to look down!"

Using all the strength she could muster, pushing up with her legs, she reached over the stone edge and grabbed a tree root.

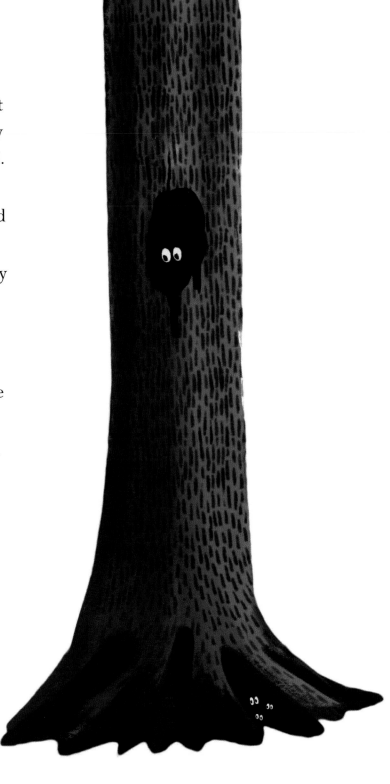

Pulling herself up, she slid over the top.

"Phew!" she thought, and so did Little Robin, who curled up on her belly with a sigh.

"Well, that was easy," she panted, smiling at him. Turning her head to one side, there it was.

"Wow!" gasped Tilly.

The two friends looked out onto the vast landscape of the Lake District. First, there were the dense thickets of Sheriff's Wood, lined with the brook which ran like a ribbon of mirrors.

Sheltered by an orchard of blossom trees was Tilly's cottage, towered over by the mountains behind. "Look, Little Robin, can you remember the names of the mountains?

Those to the left are the Langdales, and there's Helvellyn." Tilly always remembered that one, because it was her house team at school. Then below them was the village of Windermere.

All the little lights shone out of the houses, making the entire sky above them glow with a golden hue. Tilly thought how very small it looked, a tiny drop of orderly placed brick, slate, and metal set among the vast countryside.

"How very strange it is to think of all those people who live out there; their hopes, dreams, miseries, and joys in such a tiny place," she thought.

A rumbling of thunder got Tilly to her feet. "You should always take the weather very seriously. Otherwise, it would throw all sorts at your head to get some attention," she whispered.

Tilly stepped carefully across the rough surface until she came to a great crevice, which split the rock in two. There was a faint noise coming from the black void.

"Hello," called Tilly, but no answer came. It sounded like something was scratching; something very big, something very sharp. In fact, it sounded just as though a huge set of claws was scraping against the rock. It was growing louder by the second.

Little Robin was flapping his wings as hard as he could, trying to pick Tilly up. But the only thing he lifted was the hood on her raincoat.

"It's no use," Tilly whispered, without taking her eyes off the blackness.

"It's like me trying to carry an elephant on my head. Fly away, Little Robin. Quick!"

Shaking his head, he flew into her chest pocket and waited for the beast to appear.

Then out of the darkness, hooking over the rock, were two sets of sharp black claws.

Then, in one continuous movement, like a tower growing right out of the ground in front of her, the dragon appeared.

Its scales sat on top of one another like Mr. Snow's roof tiles, except that they looked like they'd been tie-dyed in art class with deep purple, vivid turquoise, and midnight black.

The dragon threw Tilly a wicked smile, showing hundreds of gleaming black teeth.

"A little bigger than you expected, am I?"

Tilly tried to stop her hands from trembling, and she could feel Little Robin's heartbeat against her chest like an egg timer going off.

"It's terribly hard to know what to do when you are facing attack. Afterward, you may think of something really clever to catch the fellow out. However, at the time, one usually behaves very foolishly, especially when faced with a ginormous dragon with razor-sharp teeth and fire breath which can cook a chicken in four seconds, flat," her mind wandered in thought.

Tilly knew she had very little time left before she herself would become brunch. The dragon knew this too, and his yellow eyes glimmered with anticipation.

Then, Tilly had an idea. Looking down at her shiny yellow Wellingtons, she remembered a story she had once heard about King Arthur and the Knights of the Round Table. Villagers used to offer fair maidens to dragons in the hope that the dragon wouldn't eat all the cattle.

"How ridiculous!" Nonetheless, Tilly addressed the dragon with her bravest voice

"Excuse me, Dragon."

The dragon lowered its huge head down so that it was looking straight at Tilly, his nose nudging her tummy.

"Yesss," he said, licking his purple lips.

"Are you upset because nobody ties up their women and leaves them, screaming as though they've been catapulted ten million metres high in the air at 2,000 miles an hour, for you to munch on?" Tilly spurted in one breath.

The dragon was a little uneasy. Tilly thought she recognised that look from somewhere. It looked as though an angry badger was trying to remove an unwanted party hat from his furry head.

"Well, I can tell from your reaction that I've hit the nail on the head. It just so happens, that's the reason I am here," she said.

The dragon peered down at the tiny girl with curly brown ringlets, which were blowing around all over the place. He looked hard at her stern round little face with big brown eyes and flushed cheeks. He inspected the short, chubby legs and arms stuck out of her petticoat, which was covered in a print of liquorice allsorts.

Drowned by her raincoat, that was more than a little too big for her, it was clear to him that the pockets were filled with biscuits and something red and feathery.

And what was that? She was holding something out in her hands. The dragon squinted.

"What have you got there?" he asked, edging closer on his claws.

"This is what I am here to give you. Lovely. Aren't they? My people call them Wellingtons."

"Hmm, they are very shiny," bellowed the dragon.

"And they're also a very cheerful colour. They'll brighten up any cave."

The dragon laughed, and the whole rock began to shake. Tilly thought she might fall over the edge, but she managed to steady herself. Perhaps, this was a bad idea, and she was going to end up as toast, after all.

She spoke in a very small voice.

"Well, I love them."

The dragon stopped laughing. "You do, eh?"

"Yes, very much so. My mother gave me them, and I think they are wonderful."

"Hmm! Well, Miss Miniature Maiden, I accept your generous gift most graciously. The reason knights used to offer their fair maidens was quite simply because they were giving up their most precious things for the good of their people. I do believe you're trying to do the same, but with these tiny shiny yellow things, which you call Wellingtons.

Since you have been most valiant, you may attempt to slay me with your weapon of choice."

"If it's all the same to you, Dragon, I'd rather we just became friends and had a cup of tea."

"Very well. It would be a lovely view if you'd like to sit on my back."

"Oh yes, please," she replied, gleaming.

"I'm Tilly Buttersworth by the way. Pleased to meet you."

"Likewise! I'm Aridyer the Eighth, but my friends call me Nigel."

Tilly had never expected that she would be sharing her flask of tea with a dragon on a Sunday afternoon.

"I guess," she thought, "life's just like that..."

• Put on your Wellington Boots and go and look for the dragon. •

Crinkle Crags

Pike 'O' Stickle

Parey Ark

Orrest Head

Windermere Lake

Elleray Wood

START
Windermere
Station

A591

Fifty pence from this copy goes to The Lake District Mountain Rescue.
We proudly support this Charity.

ISBN – 978-1-5272-5364-3

Thanks to editors – Janet Dillon and Michelle Ben

Graphic Designers – Lupa Natalia and
Samuel Abiodun Solomon (Crystal Studios)

Printed in England

Friends can be found in the
most unexpected places
- *Nigel the Dragon*